KL**a**S**K**Y
CS**U**P**O** INC.

Based on the TV series *Rugrats*® created by Arlene Klasky, Gabor Csupo, and Paul Germain as seen on NICKELODEON®

SIMON SPOTLIGHT
An imprint of Simon & Schuster
Children's Publishing Division
1230 Avenue of the Americas
New York, NY 10020

GROLIER
B O O K S

This edition published by Grolier Books.
Grolier Books is a division of Grolier Enterprises, Inc.

ISBN 0-7172-8917-6

By Gail Herman
Illustrated by Louie Del Carmen
and James Peters

Simon Spotlight/Nickelodeon

Pizza time!
Tommy and his friends
looked for the box.

That's how they always
got their pizza—in a box.
But it was different tonight.
    "We're going *out* for pizza!" said Didi.

Didi and Betty took the babies
to Pete's Pizza.
Three stray cats were in the doorway.
    "Watch out for those cats,"
Didi told the babies.
"They might scratch."
    Lil did not think so.
They looked sad!
But Betty hurried
her away.

Inside, Pete was tossing pizza dough
high in the air.
"Did you see those cats?"
Pete asked Didi and Betty.
"Someone should take them home.
They are the biggest pests around."

The *biggest* pets?
Lil thought they were kind of small.
    The babies watched Pete
toss the dough.
Up and down.
Up and down.
    Suddenly Tommy whispered,
"Hey, guys, we have to find
the *real* pizza—the kind
that comes in a box!"

Tommy spied another room.
"That must be the place!" he said.
Didi and Betty were busy.
"Now's our chance," said Tommy.
"Come on!"
"I don't know, Tommy," said Chuckie.
"Anything can be behind that door . . .
anything!"
Then Lil and Phil took Chuckie's hands,
and they all sneaked away.

Inside the room, Chuckie kept
his eyes shut.
But the other babies grinned.
What a place!

The room was full of tomatoes
and big doughy balls.

"Come on, Chuckie," said Tommy.

"Let's play ball!"

The babies played catch with the
dough and the tomatoes. *Splat!*
Flour and bits of tomato flew everywhere.
    "Look at this!" said Phil.
"It's the stuff we put on Christmas trees."
    "Let's sprinkle it!" Lil said.

Just then, Tommy saw
the stack of pizza boxes.
"Pizza!" he yelled.
But the box was empty—
all the boxes were empty!

"No pizza anywhere!" said Tommy.

Then the babies heard a loud "*Mew!*"
Chuckie jumped.

"Wh-what was that?" he asked.

"It's the big pets!" said Lil.
"Maybe they want
to come inside."

How could the babies help?
Tommy had an idea!
The babies stacked the boxes
one by one,
all the way to the window.
Tommy climbed up
and let the cats in.

The cats looked around.
They nibbled on the tomatoes.
They chewed on the doughy balls.
"Look!" cried Lil. "The pets are
eating the toys!"

The cats rolled and played and ran
and jumped with the babies.

"Now let's give the big pets a ride,"
Tommy said.

Around and around went the cats.

Crash! Boom! Bang!

FLOUR

"This is fun!" said Chuckie.
"Told you!" said Tommy.
Now what else could they do?

Just then, Pete, Didi, and Betty
hurried in.

"Oh, no!" cried Pete.
"Those big pests made a big mess!"
He was so upset, he
almost dropped
his pizza.

The babies looked at one another.
They felt bad.
They had helped to make the big mess, too.

STRING CHEESE

"Here, big pets," said Lil.
"You can play with these strings."
The cats batted the cheese,
and then gobbled it up.

"Why, they're just hungry,
the poor things!" cried Betty.

"*Mew, mew, mew . . . .*"
called the cats.

One cat licked some tomato sauce
from the pizza.

Another pulled at the cheese.

And one nibbled on the crust.

Pete smiled. "Well . . . ," he said.
"The cats are kind of cute . . .
and they like pizza!
I guess they can stay here
where it's nice and warm,
and there's plenty
to eat."

Didi looked at her watch. It was getting late.

"Oh dear," she said.

"Can we have the pizza to go?"

The babies were happy. The cats had a home, and *they* would have pizza in a box—just the way they liked it!

How To Get Cookies

"I love cookies!" Chuckie says. "And I know just where and how to get them."

- Tell the grown-ups you need cookies as medicine.
- Practice bowling, so you can win the Champion Chip (Cookie).
- Trade your Reptar Bars for cookies.
- Make yourself invisible with the vanishing cream so you can sneak into the kitchen.

Say you need cookies as "aspiration" for your painting.

Make your voice sound like a grown-up with the Pickles Voice Frequency Modulator 5000, and order cookies from Zippy's Deli.

Climb on top of each other and get cookies from the kitchen counter.

Move into a cookie factory.

Just ask your mommy or daddy to make you some!

Inside Cynthia's Brain

Angelica's doll Cynthia has to put up with a lo
Ever wonder what she's thinking?

- "I hope my hair grows back someday."
- "I've been buried in sand so many times, I'm starting to grow a shell."
- "It's really dark inside a fish."
- "Luckily, my head pops back on."
- "The toilet makes a lousy jacuzzi."
- "I want a REAL castle instead of one made out of blocks."
- "I'm all dolled up."
- "The worst way to travel? Inside Spike's mouth."
- "You know, that Reptar's kind of cute."
- "If only I could trade places with Angelica for just one day . . ."

Joke Break

What do you call Tommy's cousin after she falls in the garbage?

Ansmellyca

Knock, Knock.

Who's there?

Drool.

Drool who?

Drew'll be here soon to pick up Angelica.

What happened to the toaster when Tommy put jelly in it?

It jammed.

What's cute and fuzzy and lives at
the North Pole?
A teddy brrr.

What kind of dog is best with babies?
A Baby Setter.

What's the babies' motto?
"If at first you don't
succeed, cry, cry again."

Why should Chuckie
play basketball
someday?
Because he's already a great dribbler.

How is Spike like a
telephone?
He has a collar I.D.

How is Chuckie's nose like a teddy bear?
They're both stuffed.

What a Mess!

Sometimes we make a bit of a mess. But we're babies—and that's what babies do. There was the time when:

- Angelica made us spray a hose in the living room to make a swimming pool.

- Phil and Lil did a water ballet in the mud for the playground olympics.

- Chuckie and Tommy used mustard to wash Henry the stuffed lion.

- We pulled all the toilet paper off the roll in the bathroom.

We pushed all the garbage out of the garage for Hubert the Garbage Truck Monster to eat.

We fought over the bottle of chocolate milk—it spilled everywhere!

We ate a chocolate pie and got it all over everything.

We ate everything at the all-you-can-eat buffet in Las Vegas!

Stu's Inventions

My fine son, Stu, spends his day inventing all kinds of things, including toys. Sometimes his inventions even work!

PICKLES BABY SUSPENDERS
Locks diaper on, so babies can't get naked.

ANTI-GRAVITY PLAYPEN
This one worked great until it blew out all the electricity.

A MECHANICAL DRAGON
It's huge! Every year, Stu builds a new one for the Renaissance Fair because it somehow gets beat up.

MR. FLUFFLES CLOWN LAMP
This one worked pretty well until Angelica broke it.